The Beginner's Bible®

Super Heroes of the Bible

Sticker & Activity Book

ZONDERkidz

Copyright © 2015 by Zonderkidz

Published in Grand Rapids, Michigan, by Zonderkidz. Zonderkidz is a registered trademark of The Zondervan Corporation, L.L.C., a wholly owned subsidiary of HarperCollins Christian Publishing, Inc.

Requests for information should be addressed to customercare@harpercollins.com.

All rights reserved.

Design: Jody Langley

Printed in the U.S.A.

24 25 26 27 28 /CWM/ 20 19 18 17 16

Use the stickers to finish the picture.

Noah and the Great Flood

A long time ago, God told a man named Noah to build a boat. He needed to fill it with two of every animal. God was going to send a great flood. It would cover the whole earth. Noah's neighbors thought he was crazy! But Noah listened to God.

Trace NOAH'S name.

NOAH

Joseph's Colorful Coat

Joseph's father gave him a beautiful colored coat. But Joseph's brothers were jealous. "Why didn't *we* get new coats?" they asked. They threw Joseph into a well. Then they sold him as a slave in Egypt.

Color-By-Number

1 = Red   4 = Blue

2 = Yellow   5 = Purple

3 = Green   6 = Brown

Joseph had 12 brothers. Can you count all 12 apples?

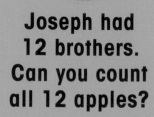

4

Use the stickers to finish the picture.

Joseph in Egypt

God turned that bad thing into a good thing! Joseph became a very important person in Egypt. He helped save all the people from going hungry when there was no food. He even gave food to his brothers!

Help baby Moses float safely to the Pharaoh's daughter.

A Baby in a Basket

To save her son, a woman gently laid her baby in a basket.
Then her daughter placed the basket in the river.

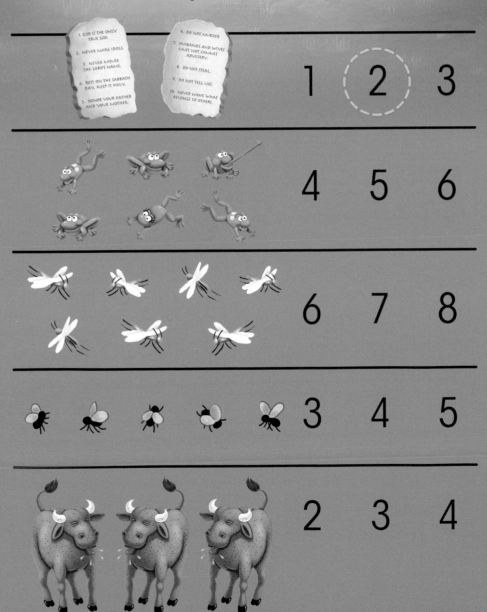

Ten Plagues

When Moses grew up, he got a wonderful message from God. God wanted Pharaoh to let his people go. But Pharaoh said, "No way!" So God sent 10 plagues.

How many are in each group?

1 **2** 3

4 5 6

6 7 8

3 4 5

2 3 4

The Battle for Jericho

Joshua was a hero because he listened to God. God told Joshua, "March your army around Jericho. Have the priests blow their horns. Do this once a day for six days. On the seventh day, have your army march around the city seven times."

Joshua did just what God said. And guess what? The walls came tumbling down!

Use the stickers to finish the pictures.

Find and circle the words in the puzzle:

Wall
Jericho
Joshua
Shout
Trumpet
Army

B	T	R	U	M	P	E	T
S	H	O	U	T	E	K	H
G	M	J	O	S	H	U	A
R	V	K	S	E	L	L	I
A	D	M	C	T	G	E	S
R	P	B	O	W	A	L	L
M	I	Y	Z	D	M	G	M
Y	J	E	R	I	C	H	O

The Long-Haired Hero

Samson was a very strong man. He saved God's people from their enemies.

Samson could lift very heavy things. Draw a line from Samson to what is heavy.

A Good Heart

David was a shepherd. He was the youngest of his brothers. David trusted God and he was able to do great things.

Use the stickers to finish the picture.

?

Look at the faces. How does each person feel?

happy

angry

scared

A

B

C

David and the Giant

David wasn't afraid to fight the giant, Goliath. He knew that God would be with him.

Look at the pictures. Write the number 1 below what happened first. Write the number 2 below what happened second. Write the number 3 below what happened third. Write the number 4 below what happened last.

11

Daniel and the Lions' Den

King Darius made a new law. For 30 days, everyone had to pray only to him. Daniel knew this was wrong. He knew that he should only pray to God. So Daniel disobeyed the king's law.

Find the differences between the two pictures. Hint: There are 6. Circle them.

Use the stickers to finish the pictures.

The king threw Daniel in the lions' den. But God sent an angel to protect Daniel! Trace and write L.

Circle the words that begin with the L sound like LION.

Legs

Lamp

Dog

Pigs

Lamb

Logs

Jonah and the Big Fish

God often spoke to Jonah. One day, God told Jonah, "Go to the big city of Nineveh. Tell them to stop doing bad things."

But Jonah ran away. He did not want to go to Nineveh. Instead he got on a boat to sail across the sea. God sent a big storm to stop Jonah. The sailors in the boat tossed Jonah overboard. Then the storm stopped, and Jonah was swallowed by a big fish!

Connect the dots to finish the picture. Then add the stickers.

14

Color Jonah and the big fish.

A Second Chance

Jonah prayed to God for forgiveness. After 3 days, the big fish spat Jonah out on dry land. This time, Jonah obeyed God. The people of Nineveh were sorry for doing bad things, so God forgave them.

With God's Help

The Bible is full of heroes. These were people who listened to God.
They may have been small, but they did big things. Circle what is bigger.

Who is your favorite Bible hero?
Why are they your favorite?

16